The Inheritance

HEIRS RESTORED

FIRST EDITION
Published in July 2022

Y.A.M. MEDIA
YANNI AYANA MEDIA, LLC
www.YanniAyana.com

ISBN: 979-8-98641 51-0-9

Library of Congress Registration
Ayana, Yanni
The Inheritance: Heirs Restored
Registration Number: TXu 2-313-998 | April 18, 2022

Category: Christian Fiction, Fantasy

Library of Congress Cataloging-in-Publication Data

Author: Yanni Ayana Media, LLC |
YAM.Books@outlook.com

Cover Design and Layout: Eli Blyden Sr. |
www.EliTheBookGuy.com

Printed in the United States of America by: A&A
Printing & Publishing | www.PrintShopCentral.com

Acknowledgements

I thank GOD for giving me the grace, wisdom, and courage to complete this book, "The Inheritance: Heirs Restored."

I would like to give a special thank you to my mother Mauva Morrison for supporting me with prayers, and love in every area of my life.

This book "The Inheritance: Heirs Restored," is my first short story in the genre of Christian fiction. God intentionally allows different people on our journey to guide us into His perfect will. I am thankful for my sister Dr. Alicia Francois, Christine Bland-Millard founder of C.L.C., Inc., and Eli, CEO of EliTheBookGuy.com for making this book a reality. We all hope that this story of redemption, will reconnect hearts back to God all over the world.

Also, a sincere thank you to my father Michael Bernard, family, loved ones, pastors, leaders, and friends.

God richly bless you.
–Yanni Ayana

*"...Tell them about ME.
Through you they will know me,
and their true identity."*

–King Sequoia

The Inheritance

HEIRS RESTORED

Written by: YANNI AYANA

Introduction

This story will reveal the loving heart of the Father for all his children. The Father's detailed plan of redemption was intended to restore the true heirs to their power, and authority through faith in His Son. My overall purpose is to help you understand your origin, identity, and authority in the Kingdom.

The Tree Kingdom

The kingdom of Arbol is a tree kingdom, which was filled with festivity, music, and joy. All the trees, which included, plants, vines, and shrubs, shared very rich soil. The citizens of Arbol enjoyed different seasons, and weather. Their kingdom also possessed treasuries of wind, rain, lightning, and hail.

Arbol's river waters were beautiful. They were crystal clear, with a shimmery, light blue sapphire-color. The surface of the mountains was decorated with diamonds, rubies, emeralds, and gemstones of every kind.

King Sequoia was a powerful, enormous tree, unmatched in size, and stature. He had large, long sturdy branches that spread as far out as the eye can see. Though he was very sovereign and majestic, he gave all his creation free-will to make decisions. He gave everyone gifts and talents with a desire to share them with each other and fill the atmosphere with love.

The citizens of Arbol reverenced King Sequoia and his family, who were also called the

Trinity. His family was his son Coast, and chief advisor Don. They were the largest trees in the eternal kingdom of Arbol and were the only trees that bore the OLIVE BRANCH seal. The OLIVE BRANCH seal at times illuminated with a bright light on the core of their trunk.

In the kingdom, there was also an evil, envious jacaranda tree named Jaccard. He was a tree with beautiful purple flowers and was admired by all who looked at him. Many trees and plants gazed at his beauty and loved his music that filled the kingdom. He was one of King Sequoia's leaders and provided music for every occasion. Jaccard was able to play sounds within himself and taught other citizens with musical talents.

Often after a celebration, Jaccard enjoyed conversations with King Sequoia's military guards called strong-keepers. However, one evening after laughter, and talking about the highlights of the festival, the meet up took a different turn when he said to the group,

"I'm no different than King Sequoia! Look at how everyone admires me in the kingdom of Arbol! There would be no joy here without my singing and music!"

The strong-keepers listened to Jaccard and pondered his words. However, not all of them were pleased with his criticism of the Royal Trinity. Yet, there were a few that agreed with him quietly in their hearts.

Earlier that same day, the Trinity met on the largest mountain called Triumph, to discuss the expansion of Arbol.

"I want to enlarge my kingdom," said King Sequoia.

"I will create an additional territory and it will be a colony. It will have some of the features, and characteristics of my eternal kingdom. However, I want my children to have dominion and rulership in my new colony called Aarde."

"Your children?" asked Coast.

"Yes Son! I want more sons and daughters" replied King Sequoia.

The Trinity locked their branches together in agreement and the OLIVE BRANCH seal on their cores began to glow brightly on their trunk. Then King Sequoia declared,

"Let us make everything now! They will be made in our image and after our likeness. They will have a physical form purposed to operate in the colony Aarde. I will call them Hyquoias, and they will be a part of our Sequoia family. The first two hyquoias will be named Almund, and Evergreen. They will be as husband and wife, to multiply, and fill the colony with hyquoia trees.

I want the hyquoias to rule Aarde the same way we govern the eternal kingdom of Arbol. They will be able to make decisions and their creativity, ideas will be inspired by ME. The hyquoias will have a loving relationship with us and fill the land with our culture, and values."

Coast, and Don were very pleased with all the plans! Then King Sequoia took a deep breath, and blew a great wind on Almund, Evergreen, and the colony Aarde. Everything suddenly, came alive and the King looked at the hyquoias with great love and adoration.

After a moment of celebration on Mount Triumph, immediately King Sequoia stepped back with anger in his eyes.

"Father, what is wrong?" asked Coast.

"Great King, you look disturbed! Is everything alright?" asked Don.

King Sequoia replied softly, "Jaccard has officially decided to exalt himself!"

* * *

In a dim-lit cave by the crystal blue river in Arbol, the rebel strong-keepers tried to negotiate a power deal with Jaccard secretly. Meanwhile, the faithful strong-keepers rushed to Mount Triumph to inform the Trinity of Jaccard's blasphemous plans.

"Jaccard! If we were to help you become king of Arbol, and overthrow King Sequoia and his holy team, what is in it for us?"

"You're telling me, you are willing to go against the MIGHTY KING SEQUOIA, COAST, DON and your fellow strong-keepers?!" Jaccard questioned sarcastically.

After a burst of hysterical laughter Jaccard shouted,

"YOU ARE ABSOLUTELY CRAZY!" His voice shifted from laughter to anger, and then intrigued with curiosity, he slowly approached them and asked,

"How do I know you are serious? Are you trying to set me up for destruction? So, you can look like heroes to the Mighty King Sequoia?"

Elm, leader of the rebel strong-keepers said,

"My brother Oak, and I will gather an army to overthrow this kingdom, but you will have to make US as powerful as you! We will be as

Coast and Don to you, in all of King Sequoia's territories!"

Jaccard chuckled and said,

"Be as Coast and Don to me?! In my kingdom, there is only ONE king! And that will be ME! However, I will give you power secondary to mine, to execute my will throughout Arbol. Your followers in your army will be subject to you. However, you both will be subject to me only! You will have power and authority over all the citizens to make them comply to my laws! That is more than what you have today as being mere military guards, oh I'm sorry! I mean strong-keepers to King Sequoia!"

Elm and Oak looked at each other, turned to Jaccard and replied,

"Yes! It's a deal! Give us some time to train and raise up an army! We will report to you when they are ready for battle!"

* * *

Meanwhile on Mount Triumph, King Sequoia said, "Coast, Don! Jaccard wants to be king and takeover my kingdom Arbol!"

Don and Coast replied, "WHAT?!"

Then Coast said, "Father, Jaccard will NEVER succeed with his plans!"

King Sequoia with a deep sigh replied, "Coast, he wants to be as powerful as we are and worshipped as I AM!"

Don rushed towards King Sequoia and said, "we must take counsel together to protect the citizens of Arbol, and the royal children in the new colony Aarde!"

King Sequoia looked at Don and Coast and said, "I declare to you both this day, that Jaccard and his followers will be destroyed forever!"

"Father, should we warn Almund and Evergreen?" asked Coast.

"They will be safe!" said King Sequoia, "If they obey the decree that I will give them. Coast, do you believe Almund, and Evergreen will obey under pressure?"

Coast replied, "Father, you know all things! I do know that you love them and will look out for them!"

Don in deep thought, and with a silent gaze; looked upon King Sequoia and said to him, "Honorable King- I will issue the decree to the hyquoias in Aarde at your command."

Almund and Evergreen loved life in the colony and their fellowship with King Sequoia, Coast, and Don. The Trinity visited the hyquoia citizens in Aarde daily. The hyquoia trees would share updates on their progress of new discoveries, and most current events.

King Sequoia would walk with them by the sea, and along the rivers to listen to their thoughts, and creativity. He loved engaging with all the hyquoias. He was so proud of them because they were so much like Him in every way! He loved being in their company and cared for his royal children.

One evening while visiting them, King Sequoia was deeply troubled in his heart. He summoned for Almund and Evergreen and asked, "Did you receive my decree from my chief adviser Don?"

Almund replied, "Yes Father! We have received your one and only decree! Don shared it and told us that this was the only command from you and that we must obey it!"

King Sequoia exhaled with a breath of relief, held Almund's and Evergreen's branches, looked them in the eyes and said solemnly,

"Obey my one decree. If you disobey, you all will die."

They both became sad by King Sequoia's words. Almund bowed before him and said,

"Oh Father, believe me! We will obey! We will obey your decree!"

* * *

In the eternal kingdom of Arbol contention filled the atmosphere.

"King Sequoia, King Sequoia! Jaccard, and one third of the strong-keepers from your kingdom has attacked the citizens and military guards of Arbol!" cried Micah, the head strong-keeper of the kingdom.

King Sequoia commanded, "Coast, Don, the time is Now! Jaccard will NOT prevail in my kingdom! Micah, release the treasuries!"

Two of the mightiest strong-keepers, Micah and Gabal opened the treasuries of lightning, thunder, wind, and hail! Large, dark swirling clouds filled the air, and the mountains shook violently! The soil crumbled, uprooting the citizens of Arbol! As they ran frantically for safety, their roots became entangled, they stumbled and fell over each other. Some were victims of stampede, yelling for help in panic, and dismay!

The rivers began to flood and overflow. The quakes that shook the ground and mountains, caused tsunamis to form in the sea. The waters became very violent, and ferocious! The large waves began crashing against the cliffs, mountains, and shores. Many trees lost their balance and fell to the ground. The other citizens in Arbol were afraid of being washed away into the sea, ran quickly to higher ground to hide in the caves, with in the mountains. Larger trees hovered over smaller trees to shield them from the lightning, wind, and hail. The dark clouds filled the kingdom and made it difficult for the citizens to see the battle between Jaccard's army and King Sequoia's strong-keepers.

"STEP DOWN KING SEQUOIA!" yelled Jaccard.

King Sequoia's eyes were as flames of fire, when he pointed to Jaccard and said,

"YOU HAVE TRULY LOST YOUR MIND JACCARD! THERE'S NO REDEMPTION FOR YOU AND YOUR BAND OF LOSERS! YOUR DESTRUCTION WILL BE ETERNAL! AFTER ALL I GAVE YOU IN MY KINGDOM! HOW

DARE YOU COME AGAINST ME LIKE THIS?!"

Jaccard then looked to the left and right of King Sequoia and shouted,

"DON, COAST, worship me, and avoid being destroyed with your KING!" He turned his evil gaze at the King and said, "Your Majesty, the hyquoias, your offspring, the ones that bear the Trinity's OLIVE BRANCH seal, YES! Your royal children…oh-I mean your royal clones in the new colony Aarde! I will make them my slaves and destroy them too! I will rule and have dominion over them, and the colony! But first I will destroy- The Trinity!"

The battle grew intense! The royal strong-keepers of Arbol battled with the band of rebels, wrestling with entangled branches. King Sequoia's strong-keepers were filled with strength and might. They threw large boulders at Jaccard's army, smashing them, and tearing off their limbs. The one-third of the strong-keepers recruited by Oak and Elm, were greatly defeated!

KING SEQUOIA stood tall and mighty, and glowed with inconsumable fire! With a voice as of thunder he said,

"JACCARD, I'VE GIVEN YOU BEAUTY, POWER, INFLUENCE, THE GIFT OF MUSIC- IN MY KINGDOM ARBOL! I ALLOWED YOU TO SHARE YOUR GIFT WITH MY CITIZENS!?! I HAVE SET AN APPOINTED TIME FOR YOU AND YOUR ARMY. ETERNAL TORTURE IN UNQUENCHING FIRE, MOST ASSUREDLY WILL BE YOUR FATE!"

As he was speaking, the Trinity glowed with fire and their OLIVE BRANCH seal illuminated bright as the sun! Then suddenly, the dark clouds thickened, and thunder clapped so loudly, that it vibrated through the entire kingdom. Micah, Gabal, and the royal strong-keepers grabbed the roots of Jaccard and his rebels, and in a flash of lightning flung them out of the kingdom of Arbol forever. They all landed in the colony of Aarde.

After Jaccard's exile, the King spoke to the citizens of Arbol:

"Jaccard and one third of my strong-keepers attempted to overthrow ME, my Son Coast, and my chief advisor Don! I AM OMNIPOTENT, OMNIPRESENT, AND ALL POWERFUL! NONE WILL EVER PREVAIL AGAINST

THE TRINITY, OR MY KINGDOM! We are ONE and will reign forever!"

The citizens of Arbol rejoiced and celebrated. The red resin from the dragon blood tree was used to soothe and cleanse their wounds. It was a healing balm for those who were broken and injured from the battle. They all cheered and shouted, "PEACE, JOY, RIGHTEOUSNESS IS RESTORED! THE TRINITY REIGNS FOREVER!"

* * *

In the colony Aarde, Jaccard and his army were no longer the powerful trees they were in Arbol. They became slimy, prickly, ugly, bumpy vines! They all lost their beauty, stature, and strength. All of Jaccard's beautiful purple flowers and branches were gone forever, yet, he still had the ability to sing and make music. King Sequoia also changed his name to KUDZU.

Frustrated and angry, Kudzu cried, "LOOK AT ME?! I'm no longer a beautiful tree! Where's my body? Where's my trunk?! I AM A VINE!!

"Listening to you! We lost everything!" said Elm!

"Yeah! We are now vines, and powerless against the Royal Children of King Sequoia in

Aarde! There are so many of them! Look at how tall and massive they are! They even look like him!" cried Oak.

Then Elm yelled in panic, "I noticed that too! Every tree in Aarde is in the likeness of King Sequoia! LOOK! They even have the OLIVE BRANCH seal on the front of their trunks just like the Trinity! Oh my gosh! They are going to destroy us!"

The rest of the vine tribe was angry with Kudzu, but remained silent because they were sore afraid, and felt helpless in the colony of Aarde.

Kudzu in deep thought, listened to Oak and Elm's rant and said, "I've heard about Aarde and King Sequoia's royal clones here! We are not punished eternally yet! Look around tribe! It's gorgeous here!"

A vine shouted a question from within the group, "Kudzu! Can you still play music?"

Kudzu looked at himself in disappointment, and said, "Not with this body! Hold on!" he closed his eyes and tried to hum a note: "Hmmm…" Kudzu's voice was deep and soothing. Excited about the sound of his voice he said, "Hold on everybody! Did you hear that?! I still got it! I can still SING!"

Elm, Oak exhaled in relief, and some of the other vines shouted with joy because Kudzu can still sing.

"Calm down everybody!" said Kudzu, "I think I know a way we can become a powerful tribe in Aarde!"

Almund, Evergreen and the hyquoia trees in the colony of Aarde was protected from the knowledge of the war. All the hyquoia trees continued to abide in their peaceful habitat and walked with dominion and authority under the guidance of the Trinity. Every evening, at the cool of the day, they awaited the royal visit by the mountain Victoria.

"Almund, Evergreen, the first born of my offspring in my colony Aarde! How are you?" asked King Sequoia as he lovingly embraced them with his huge branches. He then looked around with admiration and said,

"You have governed according to my ordinances and statutes. I see that you have maintained, dominion, authority, and order in Aarde. You have produced many hyquoias in the colony. I am very pleased. Aarde is managed as Coast, Don, and I rule our kingdom in Arbol. I am so proud of all the hyquoia trees! Remember, if you disobey my ONE decree, you will die and no longer have intimate access to ME, Coast, and Don. All hyquoias will surely die."

Almund and Evergreen said, "Father, Coast, and Don, we love you! We will never disobey the ONE decree that you gave us!"

Coast and Don looked at each other, then turned their gaze towards all the hyquoias with loving eyes, and compassion. For they knew that they did not know anything of the war in Arbol and could not comprehend the importance of obeying this one decree from King Sequoia.

When the Trinity returned to the kingdom of Arbol, King Sequoia sat on his throne and asked,

"Coast, Don, do you believe my royal children love me enough to obey me?"

Coast said, "Father, I LOVE YOU and will obey you!"

Then Don said to King Sequoia, and Coast, "Your PLAN will now go into effect immediately"

* * *

On a new day in Aarde, Evergreen was walking through the flower garden singing to them about their colors and beauty, when suddenly she noticed something very disturbing lying among the flower beds.

"EWW! What an ugly vine! Prickly, mossy, and nasty! Where did you come from? Yuck!" Evergreen said in absolute disgust.

"Where did I come from?!" Kudzu thought, "she doesn't know who I am? Evergreen, the mother of all hyquoias, doesn't know about what happened in the kingdom of Arbol?! Hmm, then Almund and the other hyquoias must not know about the war either!"

While offended at Evergreen's reaction, Kudzu was intrigued with the secret about his presence in Aarde. He thought, "Why didn't King Sequoia tell them about me or what happened?" He pondered deeply and said within himself, "Since you called me ugly, scorned me and said- Eww! You, Almund, and all in Aarde will be my servants!"

He then went back to the cave to tell the other vines about his encounter with Evergreen.

* * *

Down by the riverside, Evergreen ran back to Almund who was resting by the river.

"Almund! I just saw the ugliest vine today in the flower garden! It was slimy, mossy, nasty, and prickly! It was moving among the flowers as I sang to them!"

Almund asked, "Where did that vine come from? I know every form of life in this place!"

Evergreen replied, "I don't know? That is why I am asking you! We've never seen, produced, or named that hideous vine!"

"Ok! Let's remain calm. We can ask Father, Coast, and Don about the gross looking vine you saw today when they come to visit us this evening!" said Almund.

In the dark cave, Kudzu entered with excitement and shouted,

"Hey everybody! Why are you looking so sad? The colony of Aarde is great! The soil is rich, the water is clean, and they even have a sun that gives light to everything! It shines just as bright as King Sequoia did in Arbol! You know, being sentenced here until judgment isn't bad at all!"

"Why are you in such a good mood?" asked Elm.

"Elm," said Kudzu, "I don't think any of these royal hyquoias know about us, or about the battle in the kingdom of Arbol!"

All the vines were shocked in disbelief. Then Elm asked, "What made you think that?! Do you believe King Sequoia, Coast, and Don would let them be clueless about our new residence here?!"

Kudzu continued, "I saw Evergreen today singing in the flower garden. Then she saw me and was horrified at my appearance! She didn't know who I was, or where I came from!"

One of the vines in the regime yelled, "Did you talk to her?"

"No!" said Kudzu, "I just listened to her shout degrading comments about me and then suddenly, she ran away! You know what? I am going to go back there right now to see if she has returned. If I see her again, I will try to talk to her to see if she can hear me!"

Now, Evergreen being curious, walked back to the flower garden to look for that ugly vine again. Kudzu saw her searching for him from a distance. He thought, "she did come back to look for me! This is my chance!"

"Hi!" he said to her, but there was no answer. She just stared at him with disgust.

"Hi Evergreen! Hel-looo!" yelled Kudzu, but she continued to look at him with scorn, unable to hear him speak.

"Huh? It doesn't seem like she can hear me!" said Kudzu, he continued- "King Sequoia made it that I can't even talk to his royal clones! Wait! They can't hear me talk, maybe they can hear me sing? I still have my music! She better stop looking at me like that too! I'm not that ugly!"

Then Kudzu hummed a tune, and she hummed it right back!

"Can you hear me?" Kudzu asked, but there was no reply.

Evergreen just had a blank stare as she wondered why that tune, she heard was familiar?

"Why does she keep staring at me!" puzzled, and frustrated Kudzu hummed again with a little longer tune this time, observing her reaction.

She swayed her branches to the music and began to hum to the tune exactly as she heard it! Then she shouted in excitement,

"This is music from Father's kingdom in Arbol! Ahh! YES! He would let us hear it playing from his kingdom when he visited

Aarde! Ugh! What an ugly vine! Is this tune coming from you?"

"If she calls me another name! I swear I am going to jump up and wrap myself around her face!" thought Kudzu, he continued, "Ok, she can't hear me talk, but she can hear me when I sing. Evergreen recognizes my music from Arbol! I am about to own this colony right now! I am going to sing my way into power!"

Then Kudzu nodded yes to Evergreen and began to sing:

"Beautiful flowering Evergreen, you look at me with confusion and zeal. I know I don't have much appeal! Yet my singing- you enjoy! So, allow me if you please to put your mind at ease. I would like to share a secret with you and Almund. Trust me, don't shun me! I am not a disease!"

Evergreen sang:

"Oh, I hear you dreadful, friendly vine! You are unappealing indeed. Yet, the music you sing is so melodious, and brings so much joy to me. I will be kind to you and listen, for you seem gentle as a leaf. Please share your secret now and do be very brief."

Kudzu smiled, cleared his throat and began to sing in his most beautiful voice.

"I come from the kingdom of Arbol and have a message for you and Almund. I know your Father gave you this colony to rule, but compared to his kingdom- all the glory, you can't even fathom! He did not tell you about the war in Arbol, and how my team went from trees, to become vines. I am sure as you look at me in amazement, you may truly wonder why? I am sorry to share this with you Evergreen, but your Father King Sequoia, Coast, and Don have something very important to hide."

In shock, Evergreen looks around frantically to see who is nearby. She then saw Almund walking towards her from a distance. She shouted to him,

"ALMUND! ALMUND! Come quickly! Come hear this vine! He sings music from Arbol and says that Father, Coast, and Don has something to hide!"

"EWW! What an ugly vine! Gross!" yelled Almund. He then points to Kudzu and asked bewildered, "THIS SINGS?!"

"YES!" replied Evergreen- "Yes listen to it!"

"WAIT! Evergreen! STOP! Look at ME!" said Almund, as he wrapped his branches around her. He shouted, "EVERGREEN! REMEMBER FATHER'S DECREE!"

Kudzu looks confused and began to sing:

"A decree? Your father King Sequoia did not tell you about me but gave you a decree! Look at you Almund! You all look like Him! You all have His SEAL! Yes, HIS children indeed! Aarde! Such a glorious colony governed by HIS seed! What is this decree- your father gave you? And why- did he keep my presence in Aarde hidden from you?"

"WHO ARE YOU? You hideous vine! What is your name?" asked Almund!

Evergreen pointed to Kudzu and said, "Almund, he sings songs like the ones we heard from Arbol when Father visits! He is telling us that Father is keeping information from us! Why would Father do this?"

"Please address me without the insults Almund and Evergreen! I am beginning to think that you hyquoias are very mean! Please forgive me, I do not intend to be rude. Yes, I am vine! My name is Kudzu!"

"KUDZU?!!" shouted Almund and Evergreen.

Kudzu continued to sing:

"You are not like your Father King Sequoia, Coast, and Don! You do not know anything at all and are the least of the trees in comparison- to those in the kingdom of Arbol!"

"What are you saying?" asked Almund.

"How do you know this?" asked Evergreen.

Kudzu sang,

"It is obvious now, that you are not like King Sequoia! He doesn't want you to know all things and be as powerful as HIM. I am sorry to bring you this horrible news, I know it is disappointing and very grim. Almund, Evergreen, I am from Arbol, I can give you power to know all things. All you have to do, is sing this song with me!"

Almund pointed at Kudzu and shouted,

"THIS IS THE VINE! EVERGREEN! WE MUST OBEY FATHER'S DECREE!"

"ALMUND, IS THIS REALLY THE VINE?" asked Evergreen.

Kudzu annoyed, and frustrated began to sing:

"WHAT?! WHAT IS THIS DECREE? Did he tell you all about me?! What instructions did you receive- did it mention me? Tell me, please tell me- why does this decree cause you both to stumble, yell, and scream?"

Evergreen looked at Almund and said,

"Father's decree to Almund and I, is that we are not to sing the words of the unfamiliar vine! For if we agree, and sing with the vine, at that moment we will be separated from Arbol and will surely die!"

Kudzu shocked by the words of King Sequoia's decree, tried to look calm and began to sing:

"Oh, you will not die! You, Evergreen, and all the many hyquoias will become great like King Sequoia, Coast, and Don! If you sing my words, I promise you there will be no demise, all that will happen to you- is that you will become very, very wise!"

Evergreen pondered on his words and said, "Almund, I have hummed and danced to Kudzu's tune before you arrived, and nothing happened. Maybe Father, Coast, and Don do not want us to be as great, or greater than them in the colony of Aarde!"

Kudzu listened and thought, "Why would King Sequoia give them so much free will to reason and decide? This is my chance to harp on their foolish pride!" Then he immediately began to sing:

"I AM ALL I NEED! I AM ALL I NEED! NOW AS I SING, I AM AS WISE AND POWERFUL AS KING SEQUOIA, AND THE MIGHTY TRINITY!"

Mesmerized by the rhythm of Kudzu's tune, Almund and Evergreen repeated after him and sang:

"I AM ALL I NEED! I AM ALL I NEED! NOW AS I SING, I AM AS WISE AND POWERFUL AS KING SEQUOIA, AND THE MIGHTY TRINITY!"

Before they can repeat the lyrics, suddenly the mountains shook, the soil spewed out huge parasites. The mighty hyquoias of Aarde grew weak, and frail. The clouds overshadowed the sun, and the light grew dim and dark! There was silence!

"OH NO!" Evergreen cried,

"What has happened to us? Your roots are drying, your bark is falling off!"

"Yours too!" yelled Almund, "Our leaves are turning brown! Our branches are shriveling! Look at everyone! The hyquoia's fruit are rotting and they are all writhing in pain! Evergreen, why are these gigantic termites emerging from the soil?!"

"I don't know Almund!" said Evergreen, "Look at the water! It's turning into a thick brown sludge!"

They both panicked at the sight of the rapid destruction of Aarde due to their disobedience to King Sequoia's decree.

"Almund, I am scared! I have never felt this way before!" Evergreen wrapped her withered branches around him and cried hysterically.

"I am scared too Evergreen! Let's go! We must hide! Father will be here soon!" said Almund. He pointed at the ground and said, "Ugly Kudzu, you deceitful vine! Look at what you have DONE! I hope Father destroys you, and every creature of your kind!"

Kudzu laughed in their faces! Then with haste, went back to the cave to tell the other vines about his victory!

All the hyquoias searched for Almund and Evergreen to find out what happened to them and their colony. They were filled with anger when they found them hiding and afraid, they shouted,

"LOOK AT US! LOOK AT OUR HOME! WHAT HAVE YOU DONE? Where is Father, Coast, and Don? They are usually here by now!

Why haven't they come? Why haven't they helped us?!"

Almund and Evergreen were surrounded by frail, sickly, and angry hyquoias. They were both ashamed and speechless!

Meanwhile, Kudzu told all the vines what happened in the flower garden with Almund and Evergreen. "I deceived them!" he said proudly.

"I got them to disobey KING SEQUOIA'S only decree, and by doing that my dear friends-they transferred their power, authority, and dominion in Aarde to ME! And because you supported me, my fellow vines in the battle in Arbol, and we share the same fate of doom, I have decided to share my power in this beautiful colony Aarde with you!" declared Kudzu.

The vines cheered with shouts of joy! They proclaimed Kudzu as their sovereign leader.

Kudzu silenced them and commanded, "Now GO! Smother the light of every plant, flower, and hyquoia tree in Aarde! The birds will hunger and have no fruit, the parasites emerging from the soil will devour its nutrients, and feed on the hyquoias. Use the slime from your vines to contaminate the waters! This is just the beginning my dear vines! Since we are going to be destroyed in the eternal fire anyway, we will not suffer alone! We will make it our purpose to take King Sequoia's royal clones, His precious hyquoias into damnation with us!"

Kudzu continued, "Fellow vines, our mission in this royal colony of Aarde is to steal, kill, and destroy all forms of life! We must oppress the hyquoias and make them obedient to our commands. We are to invade their thoughts, and make them forget who they are, and their precious Royal Trinity! I now, have the power King Sequoia gave to them to rule Aarde! They will obey me and continue to betray the King who made them kings and queens. They are subject to me! I AM their ruler. All we need to do is sing our commands to them. This is the only way they can hear us!"

Elm shouted, "This is the ultimate revenge against King Sequoia!" All the vines began to sing and celebrate their victory!

The vines grew strong and spread throughout the colony. They smothered, suffocated, and choked the trees, and flowers of Aarde. Their leaves grew large and blocked the sunlight from plants and shrubs. Giant termites chewed on the branches, and barks of the hyquoias. Sounds of pain, and cries of agony echoed throughout Aarde.

King Sequoia appeared on mount Victoria where Almund and Evergreen were hiding in a dark cave. He was alone, Don and Coast were not with him.

"Almund, where are you? COME OUT from the darkness!" summoned King Sequoia.

Almund and Evergreen were frail, with patches of bark missing from their branches. Termites crawled all over them. They both clasped branches, walked out of the cave, bowed before King Sequoia and answered in a soft voice,

"We are here Father."

King Sequoia fought back tears at the sight of Almund and Evergreen. He took a deep breath and said with a voice as loud as the sound of thunder,

"YOU DISOBEYED MY ONE DECREE!"

Suddenly, in a flash of lightning, he vanished before them! A white fog filled the cave of mount Victoria. Almund and Evergreen fell to the ground and wept uncontrollably.

"KUDZU!" shouted King Sequoia as he stood at the entrance of Kudzu's cave. His voice was so deep, that it caused the walls of the cave to quake.

Struck with fear, Kudzu heard King Sequoia's voice, gasped and could not move or speak! His army of vines were petrified! They cowered and hid themselves.

King Sequoia continued, "You have deceived my children, and separated them from me! Not only will you burn forever on the day of judgment, your plans to rule Aarde, at the destruction of my children will completely FAIL!

I will redeem all hyquoias as heirs to my kingdom in Arbol, and the power, dominion, I originally gave to them will be restored! You stole their authority that I gave to THEM! Kudzu, your days are numbered and are approaching FAST!" Again, in a lightning flash, King Sequoia disappeared.

The vines in the cave began to wail and cried out, "WE'RE GONNA DIE!" Another vine shouted, "OUR FATE IS SEALED!"

Kudzu bewildered and shaken by the words of King Sequoia paused and with great rage commanded the vines, "GO DESTROY THEM ALL! CRUSH EVERY SEED, AND HYQUOIA IN AARDE!"

King Sequoia returned to the throne in Arbol with his heart overwhelmed with grief at the suffering of his royal children. The OLIVE BRANCH seal on his trunk illuminated a great light that was so bright, it could be seen from the colony of Aarde.

He ordered the strong-keepers to open the treasuries of wind, rain, and thunder upon the colony. Immediately, a great cloud appeared, and rain poured on the land. Coast and Don were near mount Victoria in Aarde awaiting a sign of a powerful, thunderous rainstorm to execute King Sequoia's royal plan.

The OLIVE BRANCH seals on their trunks shone brightly in unison with King Sequoia! As their seals glowed, he gave Coast and Don the command and said, "IT IS TIME!" He continued and asked, "Coast are you ready?

"Yes Father!" Coast replied.

King Sequoia looked at them from His throne and said, "Don, you will be with Coast to support him. You will be invisible to the hyquoias."

Don bowed reverently and replied, "Yes, my King!"

Then King Sequoia commanded, "Coast, my Son, be sure to do in Aarde, all that you hear and see me do in the realm of Arbol."

Coast replied softly, "Yes Father, I will submit to your ways. I will obey!"

* * *

During the storm Coast and Don moved throughout the colony. They had plans to teach their message all over the land.

"The Kingdom of Arbol is HERE! You are children of the Mighty King Sequoia! The Kingdom of Arbol is HERE!" declared Coast!

As the vines of Kudzu's army wrapped themselves around the hyquoias, they heard Coast's voice and was filled with fear!

"Why are you here Coast? The hyquoias are under our control now! It is not our time to be destroyed!" said the vines.

Coast turned and looked sternly at the vine who questioned his presence and said, "SILENCE! RELEASE THAT ROYAL HYQUOIA AT ONCE!"

The vine suddenly dropped off, hit the ground, and turned into ashes! The hyquoia tree exhaled and said to Coast with a sigh of relief,

"THANK YOU!" But inwardly he thought, "why did he call me 'ROYAL'?"

The other hyquoias watching nearby marveled at Coast's authority, beauty, and power! They whispered to each other, "He can't be from here? Look at Him! He's gorgeous! So strong, and powerful! He even has our OLIVE BRANCH seal on his trunk! Who is he? Where did he come from? He said something about a kingdom! Did you see how that vine dropped to the ground when he spoke to it?"

Kudzu's plans were to make the hyquoias forget their Father King Sequoia and the Trinity, causing them to rely on themselves to survive the oppression.

* * *

As time passed, Almund, Evergreen, and all the hyquoias lost connection to the kingdom of Arbol. They could not see King Sequoia anymore, and began to doubt whether the Trinity, or the kingdom of Arbol ever existed. The vines were successful in making the hyquoias forget their Royal Family, origin, and their power.

Kudzu's army sang songs about self-importance, to make them feel independent and to trust in their own strength to survive. The hyquoias became proud in their own knowledge, believed in their ability to solve their own problems, and became highly self-sufficient. The vines chanted melodiously in their minds, "I am all I need! I am all I need!"

* * *

All the hyquoias became suspicious of one another's motives. They hoarded soil, fought for territory that captured any glimmer of light from the sun, and had wars to possess the rivers with the least amount of pollution.

The hyquoias were in a brittle state, weakened by the songs of hate, division, selfishness, pride and greed, that they heard from the vines. Some of the healthier hyquoias bribed birds with their shriveled fruit, to transport more termites to the families that did not cooperate with their requests. There was a lot of bullying, and demand for respect. The most powerful hyquoias used the evil ideas sang to them by the vines, to accumulate light, soil, and water from the other citizens of Aarde. It became the world of survival of the fittest. There was a gulf between the poor, and the rich. The oppression was devastating. Kudzu's army and evil plan was to make all the hyquoias trust in themselves and self-destruct.

Unlike the vines, Coast did not have to sing to be heard by the hyquoias. They were able to communicate as in the past in Aarde, before Almund and Evergreen's disobedient act. His assignment was to help them remember their Father, their connection to the kingdom of Arbol, and to know their worth as King Sequoia's children.

Don was invisible to the hyquoias. He helped Coast travel throughout Aarde to teach them about the kingdom of Arbol. He told the hyquoias he was the Son of King Sequoia, they were also his children, and included in the family of the Trinity.

* * *

COAST'S message throughout Aarde:

"You have access to our kingdom if you believe in who I AM and my Words! Through me you can have access to the kingdom of Arbol because you are also King Sequoia's Royal offspring. He created you in His image and likeness. This is why you have our OLIVE BRANCH seal of the Trinity! You are designed with purpose, and each of you have something special to offer to make Aarde a great colony of the kingdom of Arbol!

Father created you to rule, govern, and have dominion over the colony, the same way HE rules and governs with power, and authority in Arbol. You have His heart, His standards, His character, values, principles, and morale with in you. Aarde, was a beautiful colony before Almund and Evergreen's disobedience to Father King Sequoia's one decree. They were deceived by an evil vine named Kudzu. He stole their power and dominion from all of you mighty hyquoias. I am here to restore your identity and authority in Aarde, please BELIEVE in ME and my Words!

You are not useless, sick, poor, and defeated as Kudzu wants you to believe! Believe in me, my Words, and Live! I am sent from my Father King Sequoia to save you! The King's Wisdom, and Knowledge will be with you, through his Chief Advisor called Don. You cannot see Him now. Don is empowering me with all Wisdom and Truth to fulfill Father's ultimate plan of redemption, and restoration for you."

Many hyquoias listened to his words and believed. Some questioned his message but was intrigued with his ability to perform so many miracles in the colony of Aarde! Coast healed their soil, their water, cleansed them from termites, and released them from the smothering vines of Kudzu's regime. He traveled through the colony teaching his one message! His popularity grew and he performed great wonders among the hyquoias. Many marveled at his message, authority, and power. However, the evil hyquoia trees who oppressed others with their greed, saw Coast as a threat to their prominent lifestyle and economy. Whenever Coast and Don were alone, their OLIVE BRANCH seal glowed in unison with King Sequoia, who was very pleased with their assignment.

In the cave Kudzu asked his army of vines, "Does every hyquoia believe in Coast and his teachings?"

Elm replied, "More and more are believing, and the ones that do believe no longer obey the suggestions we sing to them! They are questioning and deciding if an action is good or bad! They no longer blindly submit to the ideas in our songs anymore!"

"What is Don's role? I know he is here! What is he doing?" asked Kudzu.

Oak answered, "Well, none of us can see him, he is invisible. He seems to be guiding Coast and strengthening him on his journey in Aarde!"

"How do you know that?" asked Kudzu.

"Well, we heard Coast talking to Don privately at mount Victoria! Though we could not hear the dialogue between them, as he spoke to Don, we saw his OLIVE BRANCH seal glow with a bright light!" said Oak.

Frustrated Kudzu turned to look at his troubled army of vines and said, "Coast and Don will not diminish our power in Aarde! They are in MY territory now!

Gather our most ruthless, violent, and devious hyquoias! Tell them through songs to attack every believer in Coast!

YES! I think this will reduce the number of those who believe in his teachings. Also, tell the group of evil hyquoia trees to devise a plan to kill Coast.

Vines! You must work on your lyrics to oppose Coast's messages! Fill the hyquoia's minds with doubt, and unbelief! GO! GET OUT! GO NOW!"

As the vines dispersed, Oak and Elm had their own opinion about Kudzu's plan!

"Yeh, yeh! GO NOOOW!" said Oak, as he mocked Kudzu's commanding voice.

Elm laughed and said, "Yeah, he thinks it's so easy! He just doesn't know how hard it is to make the evil hyquoias trap Coast! He doesn't understand that Don protects him- even though we can't see him!"

"You know Elm?" said Oak, "I don't know if we can stop this take over! Those hyquoias look at Coast, his miracles, his power, his words, his glow, and they believe in Him! They believe he is King Sequoia's Son from the kingdom of Arbol!

What's even worse? Is that they believe they're King Sequoia's kids too! Like some sort of weird family reunion or something? Almund, Evergreen, all the hyquoias are starting to know who they are! It's rough! We can't control them like before, they don't obey our songs anymore! They are followers of Coast!"

Elm replied, "If Kudzu wants to destroy Coast, he is going to have to go out there and fight with the rest of us! He can't keep hiding in this cave giving us orders!"

Oak and Elm paused, looked at each other, and shouted, "GO NOOOW!" Then they laughed hysterically and went on their way.

Kudzu heard only the tail end of their conversation and decided, "I WILL join this fight! I will take care of Coast and Don myself!"

Meanwhile, discipleship increased in the land. The royal hyquoias who believed in Coast were able to receive sun light, because the darkness of the vines could not overshadow them anymore. The songs from Kudzu and his army had no power over them because Coast gave them the ability to discern their actions and recognize right from wrong. He also taught them how to pray and stay connected to the Father. Those who chose to believe in Coast and His message walked in rulership, dominion, and authority given to them by their Father King Sequoia in the colony of Aarde!

In the cave, all the vines and evil hyquoia trees attended the appointed meeting to report their observations to Kudzu.

The evil hyquoia trees said, "The believers are not afraid of us anymore! We can't bully them; they are fighting back! They are stronger than us now!"

The vines looked at each other and nodded in agreement. Then one of the vines said, "NONE of the hyquoias that are loyal to Coast listen to our songs anymore! They command us to 'BE QUIET,' and start to sing praise lyrics to King

Sequoia and Coast! We are powerless against them; we have to obey!"

Then one of the evil hyquoia trees pointed at Kudzu and shouted, "YOU LIED TO US! WE HAVE NO POWER!"

Kudzu shocked in dismay at their accusation! Oak looked at him and said, "We have a real problem as long as COAST is ALIVE!" he continued, "Kudzu do you think King Sequoia is going to let us get away with killing COAST?! YOU have set us up for TOTAL DESTRUCTION! Our time here in Aarde is DONE!"

The evil hyquoia trees listened to Oak's words and did not understand his fear and concern. They were oblivious to the appointed day of judgment that awaited Kudzu and his army of vines for their high treason in the kingdom of Arbol. They whispered among themselves, "Who is King Sequoia?! Will he destroy us too?"

Enraged with fury, Kudzu looked at them and shouted, "GO AND ATTACK COAST!"

Many hyquoias, including Almund and Evergreen enjoyed listening to Coast's messages near Mount Victoria. They were all believers of his teachings and felt a connection to him, though they did not remember the Trinity after the fall.

While Coast was teaching, a band of hyquoia trees ambushed the crowd chanting,

"I am all I need! I am all I need! Kill Coast the Son of King Sequoia and Aarde will be a paradise for me! No termites, clean soil, clear water, and light; I must kill Coast now-to receive my paradise!"

Suddenly, the ground quaked and rumbled as the evil hyquoias charged through the crowd to capture Coast. A great struggle erupted between Coast's followers and the evil hyquoia trees.

As Don saw them coming, he quickly led Coast into a cave and their OLIVE BRANCH seals began to glow! King Sequoia spoke to them and said,

"DON return to me now in Arbol! COAST, My Son everything I promised you is yours for restoring my children back to me! Do not be afraid Coast, you will be united with me soon in Arbol. The time to complete our plan has come!"

Don embraced Coast with all His might and returned to the kingdom of Arbol. At his departure, Coast's OLIVE BRANCH seal dimmed, and stopped glowing.

He then, left the cave, stood by the river, and watched the violence among the hyquoias. He saw them fall to the ground broken, and uprooted! Their branches snapped loudly, as they were torn off each other in battle. Trunks were bruised in the tussle, bark was stripped, leaving red resin stains on the ground.

Coast saw Kudzu nearby overseeing the battle and said, "Kudzu you think you have won, but the completion of my Father's plan has begun!" He then looked upward and said, "Father I will obey! I will not be afraid!"

Kudzu heard Coast's words and sang aloud, "PRESS THROUGH THE CROWD! DESTROY COAST NOW! DESTROY HIM NOW!"

Coast heard the song of the wicked command and did not run or hide. He stood strong and courageous as the evil hyquoia trees rushed towards him! They grabbed him by the branches and threw him to the ground. He was beaten with stone, and rocks of all sizes. The evil hyquoia trees stripped the bark off his trunk and branches.

Coast cried aloud in pain, "Father! Father!"

King Sequoia heard his cry! He clasped Don's branches tightly, wept in great anguish, and said, "MY SON! MY SON!"

The sharp stones wounded Coast with cuts all over his body. Red resin flowed as blood into the soil and river as they continued to batter him. Then an evil hyquoia tree raised a large boulder in the air, and with one swift blow, smashed it in Coast's trunk on the OLIVE BRANCH seal! Coast hollered, exhaled his last breath, and died.

The fighting between the believers in Coast, and the evil hyquoia trees ceased! Coast's followers collapsed in grief at his death. They were stunned, and felt helpless, at the sight of his dead body.

"COAST! COAST!" wailed King Sequoia from his throne in Arbol. The more King Sequoia cried, his anger grew stronger, and stronger!

"RELEASE THE TREASURIES OF LIGHTNING, THUNDER, QUAKES, AND HAIL!" King Sequoia commanded the strong-keepers!

Coast's body laid on the ground and his followers were overwhelmed with grief. Kudzu watched proudly, as the vines sang songs of victory. When the evil hyquoias trees began to cheer about their promised paradise, a great clap of thunder exploded in the atmosphere, the ground shook violently and began to split open!

A great storm emerged upon the colony of Aarde, unlike anything anyone has ever seen! Everyone was gripped with fear and ran frantically for shelter!

Elm and Oak looked at Kudzu and cried out, "King Sequoia is going to destroy us! We killed Coast!"

"VINES! RETREAT NOW! RETREAT NOW TO THE CAVE!" shouted Kudzu!

Lightning bolts struck most of the evil hyquoia trees that attacked and murdered Coast! They were set on fire and burned to ashes.

As the followers of Coast ran to take shelter from the storm, their wounds from the battle with the evil hyquoia trees were healed. The rain also washed the red resin from Coast's body into the soil and river. Suddenly, the waters that were brown with sludge, turned crystal clear again, and all the bugs and termites in the soil were destroyed.

The believers stopped running, lifted their gaze to the rivers, and soil, near Coast's body and was in awe! They turned around, encircled themselves around his lifeless body, closed their eyes, and began to sing,

"Our life is in Coast! Son of King Sequoia! We believe we are heirs of ARBOL, and royal children of the KING! We are designed to be powerful! We are filled with purpose & destiny!"

As the mourners sang their song around Coast, their OLIVE BRANCH seal began to glow for the first time. They were amazed at the beauty, and brightness of the light that illuminated from their trunks. The ground began to tremble and in flash Don appeared before them.

They were all frightened at the sight of Don! He was so huge and towered over the hyquoias in height and strength.

He said to them, "Don't be afraid!"

They also noticed Don's glowing OLIVE BRANCH seal and looked at him with reverence, and admiration! Without warning, a strong whirlwind blew around Coast and a thunderous voice was heard by all who stood around him.

King Sequoia said,

"COAST, you were obedient to my PLAN, taught my children WHO I AM, and MY Kingdom Arbol! You have sacrificed your life for them and for ME! Now through their faith in YOU, My Beloved Son, they will have direct access to ME!

RISE UP NOW! You have defeated death! My children who believe in you will know TRUTH and are mine forever! My heart is rejoicing My Son! Through your obedience, the rightful heirs to Arbol, and the rulers of MY colony Aarde, -has been RESTORED!"

Large rain drops fell from the sky, and the great light of King Sequoia shone brightly. Voices of the citizens in the kingdom Arbol sang 'HALLELUJAH!' with loud shouts of worship, & celebration! Coast's OLIVE BRANCH seal regained its light. Then suddenly, His branches were strengthened and expanded all around him. His wounds were instantly healed, and he raised Himself up with a mighty force before Don and his loyal hyquoias. "HE IS ALIVE!" they all cried with joy! "COAST IS ALIVE!"

Don and Coast looked at each other, smiled, and embraced! Coast, then turned to the crowd and said,

"Thank you Father! ALL your ways are perfect! I AM honored to have fulfilled your PLAN and receive all that you have given me in the Kingdom Arbol and here in Aarde!

Royal hyquoias, I introduce you to DON, who is of the Trinity in the kingdom of Arbol. He will be your helper! He has helped me accomplish the will of my Father in Aarde. Don is of my Father King Sequoia, and is of me! He will abide with you here; however, He will not be visible to all. You will know Him because you believe in ME.

All who hear, believe, and do the words of my teachings will know Don. He will dwell with you, help, comfort, and guide you in the way of TRUTH. Don will bring all my words, wisdom, and knowledge to your remembrance. He will show you how to govern yourselves as royal children of our Great and Mighty Father, King Sequoia! You will live, have dominion and power in the colony of Aarde through your faith in ME, and as children of King Sequoia! Listen to Don, lean on, and depend on Him. He will show you all the things I spoke about you and KING SEQUOIA!"

COAST looked up to the sky and said,

"Father, MY KING, you have trusted me, and evil does not have authority anymore! By your unfailing love, and mercy, your Royal children who believe in Me has been restored! Receive me Father, back to the throne, Don will keep all those who love me, and they will have access to us again forever."

Don looked at Coast, as the hyquoias were rejoicing, with singing, and dancing. After a long embrace, Coast began to ascend to the kingdom of Arbol. As he arose into the sky, he sang his goodbye for all to hear,

"I must go now, but I will return! Believe in ME, obey Don, and your authority and dominion will be sure! You are the rightful rulers of Aarde, and joint heirs with me in the kingdom of Arbol! Mighty King Sequoia is our Father, so you must be strong, courageous, and bold!"

Kudzu, his army of vines, and the evil hyquoia trees, saw a glare of bright light from within their cave! They came out and saw COAST'S ascension and heard DON'S voice cheering and singing songs of praise with the other hyquoias. The believer's OLIVE BRANCH seal glowed together as one. They sang aloud, "COAST IS

ALIVE! HE IS NOT DEAD! OUR FAITH IN HIM WILL NEVER END!"

"NOOOO! COAST IS ALIVE?! IT CAN'T BE! HOW?!" cried Kudzu! He pointed to the remaining group of evil hyquoia trees and shouted, "I saw when you killed him!"

Fear, and terror struck Kudzu and his army. The evil hyquoia trees were puzzled and in a paralyzed state.

Kudzu soon realized that King Sequoia had outwitted him. He knew that he was no longer a ruler in the colony of Aarde! Those who believed in Coast and His message was restored with authority, dominion, power, and remained in constant fellowship with the Trinity. Helplessness fell upon Kudzu's countenance. The whole army of vines stood in silence, for they knew that the day of their eternal judgment was coming soon.

In the kingdom of Arbol, COAST arrived and stood before King Sequoia, the strong-keepers and all the citizens!

"SON!" said King Sequoia, "Come sit at my Right Hand upon your throne! All that is mine, EVERYTHING I have created, is now YOURS! THANK YOU for your OBEDIENCE!"

COAST bowed before KING SEQUOIA and said,

"FATHER, THANK YOU! May ALL the royal hyquoias in the colony of Aarde, and all the citizens in the Kingdom of ARBOL, know that I LOVE the FATHER and that the FATHER loves the SON!"

COAST sat upon HIS THRONE in all HIS GLORY, BEAUTY, and MIGHT! Everyone in the Kingdom of Arbol let out a great shout of celebration. Coast looked upon them all and smiled with great delight to be home once more!

Don's new residence was in Aarde with those who believed in Coast. The King wanted him to protect, counsel, teach, comfort, and guide the royal hyquoias into their original purpose and design. Don was tasked with the assignment to help believers fulfill King Sequoia's will in Aarde and expand His royal family. King Sequoia wanted to restore all His children to their rightful place.

A dreadful silence echoed throughout the dark cave in Aarde, as the hopeless vines looked upon Kudzu. He looked around, cleared his throat and said,

"With DON here, we cannot stop COAST's message from spreading throughout Aarde! However, we can continue to influence their thoughts with doubt and unbelief! ORGANIZE! ORGANIZE YOURSELVES!" Kudzu shouted, "WE MUST HAVE ORDER! WE WILL HAVE STRATEGY!"

The vines cheered, and honored Kudzu with a roar of unity and strength. Their hope for revenge was being restored. Kudzu stood proud and said,

"Look at the evil hyquoias who are with us now! This is proof that not all hyquoia trees believe in COAST's teachings! My dear army of vines, HEAR ME! The hyquoias cannot command us or have dominion over us if they do not BELIEVE in Coast's, Don's, and King Sequoia's fairytales! APPLY PRESSURE! Sing songs that will make them self-sufficient and proud! Sing songs that will make them fearful, and doubt! Stir up anxiety, jealousy, and selfishness! OH YES! We are still in the game! This battle between us, and the Trinity is not over yet!"

The vines and evil hyquoia trees began to chant praises to Kudzu! He motioned for their attention and hushed them back to silence to conclude his speech in the cave. Kudzu reiterated his final plan of revenge against King Sequoia, Coast, Don, and the hyquoias in Aarde,

"Vines fill Aarde with songs of lies! They cannot know who they are! Never let them believe that King Sequoia is their Father, that COAST has reinstated them as joint heirs to the Kingdom of Arbol, and that they are the rightful rulers of Aarde. If all the hyquoias believe their message, they will rule over us, and we will never be able to influence them again! If they do not believe in COAST, our power and dominion in Aarde will remain- until King Sequoia's final judgment! We cannot oppress all the hyquoias, but we can still conquer some!"

Scriptural References

Genesis 1:26-28 (KJV)
God's New Family and His Original Plan

26 And God said, Let us make man in our image, after our likeness: and let them have dominion over the fish of the sea, and over the fowl of the air, and over the cattle, and over all the earth, and over every creeping thing that creepeth upon the earth.

27 So God created man in his own image, in the image of God created he him; male and female created he them.

28 And God blessed them, and God said unto them, Be fruitful, and multiply, and replenish the earth, and subdue it: and have dominion over the fish of the sea, and over the fowl of the air, and over every living thing that moveth upon the earth.

John 17:21-23 (KJV)
Jesus Prayer for Believers

21 That they all may be one; as thou, Father, art in me, and I in thee, that they also may be one in us: that the world may believe that thou hast sent me.

22 And the glory which thou gavest me I have given them; that they may be one, even as we are one:

23 I in them, and thou in me, that they may be made perfect in one; and that the world may know that thou hast sent me, and hast loved them, as thou hast loved me.

Romans 8:14-17 (KJV)
Adoption & Heirs

[14] For as many as are led by the Spirit of God, they are the sons of God.

[15] For ye have not received the spirit of bondage again to fear; but ye have received the Spirit of adoption, whereby we cry, Abba, Father.

[16] The Spirit itself beareth witness with our spirit, that we are the children of God:

[17] And if children, then heirs; heirs of God, and joint-heirs with Christ; if so be that we suffer with him, that we may be also glorified together.

Matthew 6:9-13 (KJV)
The Lord's Prayer

⁹ After this manner therefore pray ye: Our Father which art in heaven, Hallowed be thy name.

¹⁰ Thy kingdom come, Thy will be done in earth, as it is in heaven.

¹¹ Give us this day our daily bread.

¹² And forgive us our debts, as we forgive our debtors.

¹³ And lead us not into temptation, but deliver us from evil: For thine is the kingdom, and the power, and the glory, for ever. Amen.

Romans 10:9-13 (KJV)
How To Receive Salvation

⁹ That if thou shalt confess with thy mouth the Lord Jesus, and shalt believe in thine heart that God hath raised him from the dead, thou shalt be saved.

¹⁰ For with the heart man believeth unto righteousness; and with the mouth confession is made unto salvation.

¹¹ For the scripture saith, Whosoever believeth on him shall not be ashamed.

¹² For there is no difference between the Jew and the Greek: for the same Lord over all is rich unto all that call upon him.

¹³ For whosoever shall call upon the name of the Lord shall be saved.

Matthew 28:17-20 (KJV)
The Great Commission

17 And when they saw him, they worshipped him: but some doubted.

18 And Jesus came and spake unto them, saying, All power is given unto me in heaven and in earth.

19 Go ye therefore, and teach all nations, baptizing them in the name of the Father, and of the Son, and of the Holy Ghost:

20 Teaching them to observe all things whatsoever I have commanded you: and, lo, I am with you always, even unto the end of the world. Amen.

Foot Notes:

Define Arbol or **Árbol** (Spanish: *árbol*, 'tree')
Source https://en.wikipedia.org/wiki/Arbol

Define Aarde - Source
www.dictionary.cambridge.org *Translation of
aarde* in Dutch–English dictionary

Aarde- *noun*

earth [noun] the third planet in order of distance
from the Sun; the planet on which we live
earth [noun] the world as opposed to heaven
earth [noun] soil
earth [noun] dry land; the ground

**Three main types of Redwood trees:
Giant Sequoia, Coast redwood, and Dawn
redwood** - Source
https://housegrail.com/different-types-of-
redwood-trees

"In total, there are three distinct species of
Redwood trees: Coast redwood, Giant Sequoia,
and Dawn redwood. Of these three types, the
Coast redwood and Giant Sequoia are the most
widely known."

Jaccard/ Jacaranda tree - Source
https://www.gardeningknowhow.com/ornament
al/trees/jacaranda/jacaranda-tree-
information.htm

"The first time someone sees a jacaranda tree
(Jacaranda mimosifolia), they may think they've
spied something out of a fairy tale. This lovely
tree often spans the width of a front yard, and is
covered in beautiful lavender purple blooms
every spring."

Kudzu vine - Source
https://en.wikipedia.org/wiki/kudzu

Kudzu (/ˈkuːd.zuː ˈkʊd- ˈkʌd-/; also called
Japanese arrowroot or **Chinese
arrowroot**)[1][2] is a group of climbing, coiling,
and trailing deciduous perennial vines native to
much of East Asia, Southeast Asia, and some
Pacific islands,[2] but invasive in many parts of
the world, primarily North America.

The vine densely climbs over other plants and
trees and grows so rapidly that it smothers and
kills them by blocking most of the sunlight.[3]

About The Author

Yanni Ayana is the president of Yanni Ayana Media, LLC (Y.A.M.)

She is also an author, and bible teacher with a radio ministry broadcast that continues to bless people around the world. The objective of her media ministry is to teach the message of the kingdom of God with simplicity and understanding.

Yanni's love for bible stories, and storytelling is vividly expressed in her writings and bible teaching ministry. Her heart's desire is for others to have a loving relationship with God, through their faith in His Son Jesus Christ. She believes this relationship is vital, for God to fulfill his original plan and design for our lives.